DATE DUE		

The Happy-Time Circus

"Andrew! Andrew! Here it is again!" I called.

Andrew came flying in from the other room. Andrew is four. He is my little brother. I am six, going on seven. I am his big sister Karen.

"What is it? The Happy-Time Circus?" cried Andrew.

"Yup," I replied.

For a week, Andrew and I had been watching ads for the Happy-Time Circus. The circus was coming to Stamford, Con-

1

necticut. That is not too far from where we live.

"I wish we could go to the circus," said Andrew. "I have never been to a circus."

"That is because you are four," I told him. "I am almost seven. I've been to the circus. When you are as old as I am, you will have done lots of things."

"Did you go to the Happy-Time Circus?" asked Andrew.

"No," I replied, "I went to Doctor Doodle's Big Top."

Andrew and I stood in front of the TV. We watched the ad.

"Animals! Animals! Animals!" said the announcer. "Come see the elephants. Come see the lions and tigers. Come see Paddy's Trained Poodles and Biff's Trained Bears."

Andrew and I looked at each other and grinned. We love animals.

"Action! Excitement! Adventure!" the announcer went on. "See death-defying acts on the high wire. See the Cecily Sisters and their trapeze act. See the Balancing Bruno

2

Brothers. See clowns, clowns, and more clowns!"

The announcer told how you could order tickets. He said how long the circus would be in Stamford. Then the ad ended.

"Look at me!" said Andrew. He stood at one end of our playroom. Then he ran forward and did two somersaults in a row. "I could be a tumbler in the circus," he said. "Or maybe I could be a clown."

"Guess who I am," I said. I stepped carefully across the room. I held my arms out as if I needed them to help me balance.

"You're one of the Balancing Bruno Brothers," said Andrew.

"Right," I replied. "I wish I could be *in* the circus," I added.

"Me, too," said Andrew. "I want to be the man who stands in the middle of the tent and wears a top hat and tall black boots. What's he called again?"

"The ringmaster," I told Andrew importantly. That's the kind of thing you know when you are almost seven.

Just then the phone rang.

"I'll get it!" I screeched. I ran into the kitchen. Mommy was there making dinner. "Indoor voice, Karen," she reminded me. She has to remind me about that a lot.

"Okay," I answered. I picked up the phone. "Hello?" I said. "This is Karen Brewer."

"Hello, Karen Brewer. This is your father."

"Daddy!" I tried not to shout, but I couldn't help it.

4

"I'm calling," said Daddy, "because someone I know has a birthday coming up."

"Me! It's me!"

"Well, I was wondering," Daddy went on, "if you would like to do something special for your birthday. . . . This *is* Karen Brewer, isn't it?"

"Daddy!" I cried again. He likes to tease me. "Yes, this is Karen, and I *do* want to do something special."

I knew just what it was, too.

"Would you like to invite some of your friends to go to the Happy-Time Circus?" asked Daddy. "If you would, I'll get tickets."

The Happy-Time Circus? I was so surprised. That was not what I had expected Daddy to say at all.

Two of Everything

Of course, there was no way Daddy could have guessed what I wanted to do for my birthday. That was because I had not given anybody any hints. And I could tell that Daddy really wanted to take my friends and me to the circus. Daddy *loves* circuses. And he knew that I wanted to go to the Happy-Time Circus . . . but not for my birthday.

"Oh, Daddy," I said. I tried to sound excited. "Thank you. The circus would be . . . neat. But I haven't thought much about my birthday." That was a big lie. I had been thinking about my birthday forever. "Can I decide about the circus in a little while?" I asked him.

Daddy said I could take my time deciding. Then we hung up the phone. I went to my bedroom. I took Emily Junior out of her cage and put her on my lap. Emily Junior is my rat. (She is named after my adopted sister.)

I sat and thought. I thought about my birthday and the circus and being a two-two.

What is a two-two? A two-two is someone like Andrew and me who has two of everything because their parents are divorced. I got the name from a book my teacher read to our class. It was called *Jacob Two-Two Meets the Hooded Fang.* I thought "two-two" described my brother and me perfectly. I am Karen Two-Two. Andrew is Andrew Two-Two.

See, a long time ago my mommy and daddy used to be married. Then they got divorced. Then they each got married again.

Mommy married Seth. He is my stepfather. Daddy married Elizabeth. She is my step-mother. Andrew and I live with Mommy and Seth most of the time. But every other weekend, and for two weeks during the summer, we live with Daddy and Elizabeth.

Mommy and Seth live in a little house. No one else lives there except Andrew and me, and Rocky and Midgie and Emily Junior. (Rocky and Midgie are Seth's cat and dog.) The little house is usually quiet.

Daddy and Elizabeth live in a huge house. It is a mansion. And it is noisy because lots of people are always around. For one thing, Elizabeth has four kids of her own. They are Sam and Charlie, who are so big they're in high school, and Kristy, who is thirteen and one of my most favorite people. (She is a good baby-sitter as well as a nice stepsister.) There is also David Michael. He's seven. As soon as I have my birthday, we'll be the same age. Then there is Emily Michelle. She's the one I named my rat after. Daddy and Elizabeth adopted her.

She is two years old and came from a faraway country called Vietnam. Last but not least, there is Nannie. She is Elizabeth's mother, which makes her my step-grandmother. She helps take care of all of us. Oh, I almost forgot. There are also two pets — Shannon, David Michael's puppy, and Boo-Boo, Daddy's fat, mean cat.

Andrew and I have everything we need at each house. We have toys at each house. We have bicycles at each house. We have clothes and friends and mommies and daddies and stuffed animals at each house. Two of everything. That is why we are two-twos.

Being a two-two might sound like fun, and it can be. But here is one thing I do not like about being a two-two: I never get to see everybody in my *whole* family at once. I either see the little-house family or the big-house family. So what I had decided I wanted for my birthday was to invite all the people at the little house and all the people at the big house to one party. I just wanted us to be together.

That was why I didn't sound so happy when Daddy asked if I wanted to take some of my friends to the Happy-Time Circus. It meant that once again Daddy was planning one party and Mommy was planning another.

And that was not what I wanted.

"Somebody Come Get Me!"

Turning seven must make you awfully grown up. Last year, when I turned six, all I wanted was parties and presents. I wanted the magician and the pony rides that Daddy said he would get, and I wanted the special birthday dinner at Klunko Clown's Palace that Mommy offered me. And I wanted dolls and a Speed-O Racer and new jeans and a stuffed turtle and an awful lot of other things. But this year all I wanted was my two families together — like we were really one family.

12

Lately, Mommy and Daddy don't even talk to each other much. And they both live right here in Stoneybrook, Connecticut. You'd think they would call each other more often.

If they did, maybe we wouldn't have problems like the one we had two weeks ago. It was a Friday. Every other Friday, right before dinner, Mommy drives Andrew and me to the big house for the weekend. On that Friday, my second-grade class had been on a field trip. A bus had driven us all the way to Stamford to go to a museum. We had even gotten to eat lunch at a McDonald's restaurant. By the time we came back, it was late. School was over. All the kids and teachers had gone home. But our mommies and daddies were waiting to pick us up.

Except for mine.

Mommy was not waiting and neither was Daddy. No one was there for me. At last, only my teacher, Ms. Colman, and I were standing in the school parking lot.

"Who is supposed to pick you up?" Ms.

Colman asked. She held my hand so I wouldn't feel so bad.

"I'm not sure," I replied.

"Well, let's go inside and I'll call your parents."

Ms. Colman led me into our dark, empty school. I wanted to cry out, "Somebody come get me!" but I didn't. I didn't have to. Ms. Colman talked to my parents. It turned out that Mommy thought Daddy was going to pick me up since I was going to his house for the weekend anyway. And Daddy thought Mommy was going to pick me up since she had to bring Andrew over to the big house anyway.

I felt like nobody cared about me. My feelings were hurt. And that was why I wanted my two families to be more like one family.

I was sitting on my bed, holding Emily Junior, when Mommy came into my room. She was smiling.

"Honey," she said, "I've been thinking. Your birthday is coming up, and seven is a pretty grown-up age."

"Yup," I said, grinning. Had Mommy guessed what I wanted to do?

"So, how would you like to have a fancy dinner right here at home? Just you and Andrew and Seth and me. We'll eat in the dining room, we'll use our best china, we'll even have candles. A formal, grown-up supper."

I couldn't believe it! "No!" I howled. I started to cry. "I don't want just us. I want Daddy and my other family, too."

Mommy looked thoughtful. Finally she said, "Karen, I don't think that's a very good idea. For one thing, we can't fit that many people around our table."

"Then Daddy will take us all to the circus," I said. "He could pay for the tickets. I know he could." And that way, I thought, my two families could be together. Plus, we would have fun!

But Mommy looked very hurt. "I'm sorry," she said. "I'm sorry I can't afford to give you as fancy a party as your father can. We'll talk about your birthday another time."

Then she left the room.

I started to cry again.

Karen's Big Ideas

Mommy and I had our argument on a Thursday. The next day was a going-to-Daddy's Friday. After school, Andrew and I packed our knapsacks. We never have to take much over to Daddy's since we are two-twos.

While I was packing, Mommy came into my room. I knew she wasn't mad at me. She never stays mad long.

"Karen," she began, "about your birthday — "

I know I'm not supposed to interrupt

17

people, especially grown-ups, but I did anyway. "Mommy," I said, "don't worry about it. Let's not talk about my birthday now. We can talk on Sunday night when Andrew and I come home. I need to think about some things." The truth was that I was getting a big idea, but I wanted to talk to Daddy about it first.

"Okay," said Mommy, and she gave me a kiss.

"You won't forget to take care of Emily Junior while I'm gone, will you?" I asked.

"Of course not. Seth and I know just what to feed her."

"Will you play with her every day, too? She needs exercise."

Mommy paused. "Well . . . Seth will play with her." Mommy doesn't really like rats. So she had been *very* nice when she'd said I could get one.

"That will be fine," I told her. "Thank you."

An hour later, Mommy was dropping

Andrew and me off at the big house.

" 'Bye!" we called to her.

"See you Sunday, alligators," she replied.

Mommy is so silly.

The door to the big house opened before Andrew and I had even reached the front porch. There was Kristy! Behind her were Daddy and Elizabeth and Emily Michelle and David Michael and Sam and Charlie and Nannie.

Andrew and I ran to them and started hugging everybody.

Nannie said, "I'm so glad to see you!"

Daddy said, "I love you!"

And Emily Michelle said, "Hi, *hi*, HI!" (She doesn't talk much yet.)

Sometimes, evenings at the big house are quiet because all the grown-ups go out and Kristy sits for us kids. But that night, everyone was at home. We sat around the table in the dining room. The dining room is huge. So is the table. Lots of people could fit around it.

"You know what?" I said while we were

eating dinner. "It is so, so nice to have two families. I love everyone very much."

"Oh, yuck," replied David Michael.

He is a big pain.

I ignored him. "Daddy," I said, "I've been thinking about my birthday. You know what I want to do? Since I love everyone in my families so much, I want all of us — Mommy and Seth, too — to go to the circus instead of me and my friends."

Daddy opened his mouth, but I rushed on. "And then," I said, "we could come home and have a big, um, formal dinner. Mommy could cook it, but we would eat it here, where everyone can fit." There, I thought. That ought to make Mommy and Daddy *both* happy. We could go to the circus for Daddy, *and* have Mommy's special dinner. And my two families would be together.

But nobody liked the idea. Daddy said, "I think your mother and Seth want to give you a party of their own."

20

And David Michael sang, "Greedy-greedy-greedy-guts!"

And Sam, who likes to tease, said, "Is there anything *else* you want, Karen? A horse? A swimming pool? A new house?"

I looked at Kristy. She was frowning at me.

What had I done wrong? I was just trying to make everyone happy.

Hannie's Wedding

On Saturday morning I was feeling mad at the people in the big house. No one had liked my birthday idea. Sam had teased me, Kristy had frowned at me, and David Michael had called me "greedy-guts."

I decided I didn't want to play with any of those people. I wanted to play with someone nice. So I called Hannie Papadakis. Hannie is my big-house best friend. She lives across the street and one house down from Daddy. I have a little-house best friend, too. Her name is Nancy Dawes. She lives right next door to Mommy. Hannie and Nancy and I are all in Ms. Colman's class at school.

"Hannie?" I said when I called her that morning. "It's me, Karen."

"Hi, Karen!" replied Hannie. She sounded very excited. "Where are you? At your mom's house or your dad's house?"

"I'm at Daddy's," I told her.

"Oh, goody. Can I come over?"

"Yup. That's why I was calling. To invite you over."

"Okay. I'll be right there. I have some important news."

Hannie and I hung up the phone. I sat on our front porch and waited. Shannon sat with me. I felt very happy about that. Shannon is David Michael's puppy. She's usually with him. Or else she is asleep.

I watched Hannie's house. Soon her front door opened and she ran out. She ran all the way to the street. When she reached the sidewalk, she stopped to check for cars. Then she ran to our steps.

"Hi, Karen," she said. "Guess what. I am going to get married!"

"You are?!" I exclaimed.

"Yup," Hannie replied. She was too excited to sit down. She danced around in front of me.

"Who are you going to marry?" I asked her.

"Scott Hsu. You know. That new boy down the street. Yesterday afternoon I decided I'm in love with him."

"Wow," I said. I didn't know anybody else our age who was in love and going to get married. "When will the wedding be?" I asked.

"I'm not sure. I haven't told Scott about it yet. He doesn't know me. But I have decided what I'm going to wear — Mommy's wedding dress."

"Your mother still has her wedding dress?" I said.

Hannie nodded.

Suddenly I jumped up. "You know what?" I said. "If your mother has her wedding dress, I bet my mother has hers, too. And if she does . . . maybe she and Daddy could get married again! Then Mommy and Daddy and Andrew and I could have our old family back. Just like before the divorce."

"Yeah . . ." replied Hannie slowly.

"But first," I went on, "I've got to get Mommy and Daddy together again. They hardly even talk to each other anymore. We have to think of some ways to get them to talk on the phone. That would be a start.

After that, they'll see each other a few times, and then they'll decide to get married again."

"Maybe Scott and I could get married when they do."

"Oh, my gosh!" I cried. "That would be perfect! A double wedding! Hannie, we have plans to make."

Hannie and I planned ways to get Mommy and Daddy together. Then we planned the two weddings. It was an exciting morning.

Karen's Birthday List

Hannie and I had some very good ideas that morning. Hannie was going to introduce herself to Scott as soon as possible. She was going to go over to his house and say, "Hi. My name is Hannie Papadakis. I live right down the street. Do you want to be friends?" Then she was going to try to play with Scott every day after school. When they knew each other pretty well, she was going to say, "Let's get married, okay? I've got a wedding dress. Do you have a suit?"

I was going to take pictures at the big double wedding.

Hannie and I had some ideas for Mommy and Daddy, too.

"First," I said, "they have to talk to each other some more. You know what always makes them talk?"

"What?" asked Hannie.

"A problem. Like when I needed glasses." (I have to wear glasses. I have one pair for reading and writing, and another pair for the rest of the time.) "Or when Andrew had all those bad dreams. Or when Daddy wanted to take Andrew and me on a trip to Washington, D.C., and Mommy didn't want us to go."

"So you need to think of a problem?" said Hannie.

"I already have one," I said. "My birthday. It isn't even here yet, and Mommy and Daddy and *everyone* are mad at me." I told Hannie what was happening with my parties. "David Michael called me 'greedy-guts,' " I added. "I bet if I looked *really* greedy, Daddy and Mommy would have a phone call about me."

"What do you mean?" asked Hannie.

"I haven't written my birthday lists," I told her. "Each year, I make two lists, one for Mommy and one for Daddy. This year, I will make one list. I will give it to Daddy today. It will be so long that I will look like a *real* greedy-guts, and I bet Daddy will telephone Mommy."

"You don't want your parents to be mad at you, do you?" asked Hannie.

"Not really," I replied. "But if it will help them to get married again, then I don't care. I will stop acting greedy right after the wedding."

"The *double* wedding," Hannie corrected me.

"The double wedding," I repeated.

Hannie and I did not spend the afternoon together. We were too busy. Hannie had to introduce herself to Scott and see if he wanted to play, and I had some work to do in my room.

I closed the door and sat down at my table. On the table were some pieces of paper and some pencils. I pulled a piece of paper in front of me. On the top I wrote: KAREN'S BIRTHDAY LIST. First I wrote down the things I really did want: a stuffed ostrich, a plaid bow for my hair, a Little Miss Georgine doll, a go-cart, and all of the books by Roald Dahl, especially the one called *Matilda*. Then I tried to think of some other things for my list. I didn't really want anything else, but I added a new dress, a toy for Emily Junior, pink knee socks, and a pencil box.

The list wasn't nearly long enough, so I wrote down the title of every good book that I'd taken out of the library. It *still* wasn't long enough, so finally I had to go find the Sears catalogue. I brought it in to my room. I turned to the toy section. There. I found

page after page of games and toys. I copied down their names, even though I had not heard of most of them.

When I was finished, I had used up four sheets of paper, front and back. I had listed two hundred and twelve gifts. I gave the list to Daddy.

His mouth dropped open.

He called Mommy that night.

But the next day he did not say anything about getting married. He just looked sort of cross.

32

Karen's Accident

"Your turn, Hannie!" called Nancy Dawes.

Hannie threw her stone. It landed on the third square. Hop, hop, hop, hop *over*, land on two feet, hop . . .

It was recess time at school on the Wednesday after I gave Daddy my birthday list. Hannie and Nancy and I were playing hopscotch.

Hannie finished her turn. I was next. I threw my special hopscotch stone. The stone is so special that I keep it in my desk and only use it for hopscotch.

Just as I threw my stone, Hannie said, "I've played with Scott three times now."

"What?" I replied. I tried to turn around while I was hopping — and I slipped on some gravel and fell.

"Ow! Ow!" I cried. I clutched my knee. When I took my hand away, there was blood on it. There was blood all over my knee, too, and I had torn a big hole in my tights.

"Ms. Colman! Ms. Colman!" Nancy cried.

Our teacher came running. So did nearly all the kids on the playground. They crowded around me. My knee hurt an awful lot, but I *did* like getting all the attention. Everyone was saying, "Are you okay, Karen?" Or, "What happened?" Or, "How much does it hurt?"

I felt very special.

Ms. Colman helped me inside and down the hall to the nurse's office. The nurse took a look at my knee. She washed it out.

"Hmm," she said. "I think there's some gravel in your knee. I'd like you to see your doctor. Where can I call your mother?"

"At work," I told her. (Mommy works on the mornings that Andrew goes to pre-school.) I gave the nurse Mommy's number. Then the nurse helped me to lie down on a cot.

When the nurse left me alone, I looked around the room. The first thing I saw was . . . a telephone. Suddenly I got an idea. I hobbled over to the phone. I picked up the receiver and dialed a number.

"Hello, Daddy?" I said. "It's me, Karen." I made my voice sound tearful and sniffly. "Guess what. I fell on the playground and there's gravel in my knee and the nurse says a doctor should look at it."

Daddy didn't even ask any questions. "I'll be right there," was all he said.

Mommy and Daddy arrived at the nurse's office at almost the same time.

"What are you doing here?" they both asked, as Daddy walked into the office.

Then they both answered, "I got a call to come get Karen."

I almost giggled. But Mommy and Daddy looked very stern.

"Who called you?" Daddy asked Mommy.

"The nurse," she replied. "Who called you?"

"Karen," Daddy replied.

My parents looked at me. "Well?" they said.

"I — I just needed you," I told them. "I needed both of you."

Why did my parents look so angry?

36

"Karen," said Mommy, "when you're living with me, then you rely on me. You only call Daddy in an *emergency*. Do you understand?"

I nodded. I tried not to cry. But I felt better as Daddy carried me to Mommy's car. He and Mommy talked the whole way. They were talking about me and what I'd done and the birthday list. They didn't sound too happy with me. But that was okay. At least they were talking.

They even called "Good-bye!" to each other as Daddy left for work, and Mommy and I left for the doctor's office.

Old Pictures

The doctor did find some gravel in my knee. It hurt a lot when she took it out, and I yelled, "Ow! Stop it!" But then she put a *big* bandage on my knee and even gave me a piece of butterscotch candy. I liked the bandage very, very much. I liked the candy, too.

By Saturday, my knee was so much better that I didn't even need the bandage anymore. I took it off and let everyone see my wound. Most people said, "Ew, gross," but Andrew said, "Cool!"

Saturday was a rainy day. I didn't feel like going outside. So I decided to work on one of the plans Hannie and I had made. Mommy and Daddy hadn't spoken to each other since they came to school when I hurt my knee. It was time for them to start thinking about their wedding. So I went up to the attic in the little house. I was looking for two things — Mommy's wedding dress, and an album of the pictures that had been taken at their wedding. I'd never seen the album, but Hannie said her parents had one. She said they kept it right out on the coffee table in their living room. Hannie had been looking at it a lot lately to see how her wedding with Scott should go.

She had already decided what she and Scott would need: the wedding dress, Scott's suit, a cake, flowers, a flower girl, two bridesmaids, two ushers, a photographer (that would be me), a minister, and guests. I thought that sounded like an awful lot.

I climbed the stairs to our attic. I turned

on the light. The attic was cold, so I had to go back to my room to get a sweater. Then I returned to the attic.

I just love attics. You never know what you'll find in them. I looked around ours. I hadn't been there in awhile. The first thing I saw was my old tricycle. I rode it around. Then I found a box full of baby toys. I poked through them. Why was Mommy saving them? Next I found Eugene. Eugene was a gigantic doll my grandparents had given me. I had never liked Eugene much. I sat him in a corner.

Okay. It was time to find the wedding album and Mommy's dress. The album was easy to find. It was sitting right on a shelf. But I could not find the dress. I looked and looked. Finally I decided I was wasting time.

I forgot about the dress. I took the album downstairs. I sat on the living room couch and flipped through it. When I came to the pages that showed Mommy and Daddy kissing each other and laughing and eating wedding cake, I put the book on the coffee

table. I left it open. Then I left the room.

Five minutes later I heard Seth exclaim, "Lisa! What *is* this?"

(Lisa is Mommy.)

"What?" cried Mommy. She ran into the living room.

"This," said Seth. He sounded angry.

I peeped into the living room. I watched Mommy and Seth.

"I'm sorry," said Mommy. "I don't know how it got there. But *I* didn't — " Mommy looked up then and saw me. "Karen?" she said. "Do you know anything about this?"

"Well, I — " I began. "I put it there."

"The pictures of Daddy's and my wedding? *Why?*" asked Mommy.

"I don't know," I said. I had thought Mommy would be able to figure it out. Didn't she see that she and *Daddy* should be married?

"Young lady," said Mommy. (She only says that when she is good and mad.) "If I were you, I would remember that your birthday is around the corner. Lately I don't understand some of the things you have been doing. I suggest that you *shape up.*"

I nodded. Then I went to my room. I didn't understand Mommy, either. What did my birthday have to do with anything? And why couldn't she and Daddy see that they should be married again?

Parents are very confusing. They are unfair, too.

The Biggest
Birthday Party Ever

I did not know what to do. I took Emily Junior out of her cage. I played with her for awhile. I like to watch her nose. When she twitches it, her whiskers twitch, too. Emily Junior is always sniffing, sniffing, sniffing.

While Emily Junior sniffed around my room, I thought about Mommy and Daddy. I thought about Seth and Elizabeth. I thought about my birthday. I just had to get my two families together. That way Mommy and Daddy would have to talk to each other. And I could spend the day with all of my brothers and sisters, my parents and step-parents, and Nannie.

But — Daddy had said he wanted to take me to the circus. Mommy had said she wanted to give me a grown-up dinner. If I wanted Mommy and Daddy to be happy, I would have to go ahead with my plans for a gigundo birthday — the circus and a dinner with both my families. I didn't care if I looked like a greedy-guts. After all, it was *my* birthday, wasn't it?

There was only one thing to do. I would have to plan my own party.

I sat down at my desk. I found some paper and crayons. On one piece of paper, I wrote:

COME TO THE BIGGEST BIRTHDAY PARTY EVER! SEE THE CIRCUS! HAVE A SPECIAL DINNER (at Daddy's)! BRING YOUR PRESENTS! KAREN IS TURNING SEVEN!

Then I wrote down the date of the party and the time it would start. I said we should meet at the circus. I even drew a picture of a clown.

When I was finished, I decided the invitation looked very nice. So I made lots more until there were enough for Mommy, Seth, Andrew, Daddy, Elizabeth, Kristy, Sam, Charlie, David Michael, Emily Michelle, and Nannie. I wanted to invite Hannie and Nancy, but I decided not to. This was just a party for my two families.

I put the invitations in envelopes. Then I addressed them and stuck stamps on them.

My invitations were ready to go. All I had to do was walk down the street and drop them in the mailbox. So I put Emily Junior back in her cage. I left my room. As I passed Andrew's room, I noticed that his door was closed. He had hung a sign on the knob. It said DO NOT DISTURB. Andrew had been in his room a lot lately. And the sign had been up a lot lately.

I wondered what he was doing.

Trouble!

Uh-oh.

I was in trouble. At least I was pretty sure I was. Nobody had punished me, but nobody was very happy with me, either.

It started when Daddy and the people at the big house got their invitations to my birthday. Even though I had mailed all the invitations at the same time, the little-house invitations had not arrived yet.

You know the mail.

Anyway, Daddy spoiled my surprise. He spoiled it by calling Mommy as soon as he opened his invitation. It was Tuesday night. Dinner was over. Seth and Andrew were in Andrew's room. The DO NOT DISTURB sign was on the doorknob again. Mommy and I were in the kitchen. We were sitting at the table. I was doing some pages in my reading workbook. Mommy was paying bills.

When the phone rang, I let Mommy answer it. Usually I yell, "I'll get it!" But Mommy was right next to the phone. Besides, I was almost done with the page about vowel sounds. As soon as I finished it, I had only one more page to go. Then my homework would be done.

"Hello?" said Mommy. She paused. Then she said. "Oh, hi!" She put her hand over the receiver. "It's Daddy," she told me.

I grinned. Good! Mommy and Daddy were talking on the phone. Maybe Mommy had been thinking about their wedding pictures and they would get married again soon.

"What?!" exclaimed Mommy. "She did *what?*"

I stopped daydreaming. Mommy sounded angry.

"I can't believe she did that," said Mommy. "You *all* received invitations? . . . No, we haven't gotten any." Mommy looked *very* crossly at me. Then her cross look changed to a different kind of look. "Ex*cuse* me?" she said. "Raising a *brat?* I'm not the only one raising Karen and Andrew. You are raising them too, you know. Hold on just a minute." Mommy looked at me again. "Karen, would you please leave the room?" she said.

"But I'm not finished with my homework," I replied.

"*Karen.*"

"Okay, okay."

I left the kitchen. I stood in the dining room. Mommy had not said how *far* I had to go. I listened to the rest of her conversation. She and Daddy had a fight. And

they had it about me. I could tell by the things I heard Mommy say. They were mad. They said I was greedy. They said I was spoiled. And they blamed each other.

What had gone wrong? I had not meant to make Mommy and Daddy have a fight.

The next day the little-house invitations arrived. Mommy called Daddy. They had another argument. I listened to Mommy's end of the fight from under the table in the dining room. As soon as Mommy was done yelling at Daddy, she called a friend of hers.

"Pam?" she said. "I'm worried about Karen." Mommy told Pam everything. She told her about my birthday list. She told her about the invitations and the wedding album and calling Daddy when I hurt my knee. "I thought Karen had adjusted to the divorce and to Seth," Mommy said to Pam. "But now I don't know. I don't know at all. And her father and I are blaming each other."

I crawled out from under the table. I went into the living room. No one was there, so

I sat down in a chair and thought. All I wanted was for my two families to be together on my birthday . . . and for Mommy and Daddy to get married again. But no one seemed to understand.

Sometimes it is not easy being six. Or having parents who are divorced.

A Talk With Kristy

I wandered upstairs to my bedroom. I passed the DO NOT DISTURB sign again. I still did not know what Andrew and Seth were doing.

When I got to my room, I took Emily Junior out of her cage. I put her on the floor.

Sniff, sniff, sniff. Twitch, twitch, twitch.

"I wish you could talk," I said to Emily. "If you were Nicodemus from *Mrs. Frisby and the Rats of NIMH*, I bet you'd talk to me."

Emily poked her nose into my closet. Then she crept inside. She sniffed at my shoes and all the junk I had thrown on the floor.

"Talk to me, Emily," I said. But Emily just wanted to explore my closet. So I put her back in her cage. I went downstairs. Mommy was not on the phone anymore. She was in the living room.

"Mother," I said, "I need to make a phone call. And I would like some privacy, please. I am going to close the door to the kitchen."

Mommy looked surprised. "All right," she said.

I closed myself into the kitchen. I dialed the number of the big house.

A voice answered the phone. It said, "Brewer and Thomas Summer Home. Some are home, some are not."

I knew it was Sam. He is always goof-calling and playing tricks.

"Very funny, Sam," I said. "This is Karen."

"Karen? Karen who?"

"Karen *Brewer*. Your sister. Can I please talk to Kristy?"

"I don't know. Can you?"

"Sa-am. Puh-*lease?*"

"Okay. Here she is."

"Hi," I said, when Kristy got on the phone. "It's me, Karen. Your sister," I added, just in case. "I need to talk to you." Kristy and I usually talk twice a week when I'm at the little house.

"What's up?" asked Kristy.

"Mommy and Daddy are mad at me," I told her.

"I'm not surprised," said Kristy. "You should have seen your father's face when we got the invitations yesterday. He's upset about the party."

"But I thought the party was a good idea."

"Karen, I have never seen anyone who wanted as much for one birthday as you do. The circus, the dinner — and two hundred and twelve presents. Everyone is so mad you'll be lucky if you get *any* presents. I can't believe you actually put 'Bring your presents' on the invitations. That is so tacky."

Maybe I shouldn't have added that line. But . . .

How could I explain to Kristy what I *really* wanted? It is hard to talk to someone who's cross with you.

What I wanted didn't have anything to do with presents. I just wanted to see my families together on my birthday. And then, of course, I wanted the wedding. But that could wait.

"Oh, Kristy, you don't understand anything!" I cried. Then I hung up the phone without saying good-bye. I felt worse than ever.

I marched into the living room. "GOOD NIGHT!" I yelled at Mommy.

I marched upstairs. "GOOD NIGHT!" I yelled to Andrew and Seth.

I marched into my room. I closed my door. I put on my nightgown and got into bed. But I could not fall asleep. I could hear

Emily Junior rustling around in her cage. I guess she could not sleep, either.

So I sang the saddest song I knew in the saddest voice I could make. I sung it over and over until Emily Junior and I were both asleep.

Scott Dumps Hannie

Usually I like going-to-Daddy's weekends. But not this time.

Everyone thought I was a greedy-guts. So I was gigundo mad at them. They did not understand a thing.

On Saturday I called Hannie. Her mother answered the phone.

"Hannie isn't here," said Mrs. Papadakis. "She's at Scott Hsu's. Why don't you go over there? I'm sure Hannie and Scott would be glad to see you."

At least *some*one would be glad to see me, I thought.

"Thank you," I told Mrs. Papadakis.

I decided to leave right away. "I'm going to Scott Hsu's!" I yelled as I left the house. I did not think anyone cared.

I had never met Scott, but Hannie had pointed out his house to me several times. "That's where *he* lives," she would say. Then she would sigh deeply.

"How does it feel to be in love?" I would ask her.

"It feels . . . wonderful."

I was halfway to Scott's house when I saw someone coming toward me. The person got closer and closer.

It was Hannie.

"Hannie!" I cried. "Hi! I'm here for the weekend."

Hannie didn't answer me. She looked upset.

"What's wrong?" I asked.

"Scott does not want to marry me."

"He doesn't?"

Hannie shook her head. "No. We were such good friends, too. We were playing together almost every day. I gave Scott some Oreos once, and he gave me a caterpillar. Then today I told him I was thinking about weddings. I told him about my mother's dress and about flowers and everything."

"Did you tell him about double weddings?" I asked.

"Yup." Hannie nodded. I had turned around and we were walking back to our houses.

"Then," Hannie went on, "I said, 'Scott, we are such good friends now, I think we should get married.' And he said, 'Are you kidding?' And I said, 'No.' And he said, 'We are not old enough to get married.' And I said, 'But I'm in love with you.' And you know what Scott did?"

I shook my head. "No. What?" I was fascinated.

"He said, 'Ew, gross.' And then his brother

started singing, 'Hannie and Scott, sitting in a tree. K-I-S-S-I-N-G.' "

"First comes love," I continued, "then comes marriage — "

"Karen, you don't have to finish the song," said Hannie. "I know it myself, thank you."

Boy, everyone sure was grouchy.

"Then what happened?" I asked.

"Then Scott and his brother ran around to their backyard and I left."

"You left?" I repeated. "Without finding out if Scott loves you?"

"He doesn't love me," said Hannie.

"But he gave you a caterpillar."

"Friends give each other things sometimes. It does not mean they are in love."

"Oh." I kicked a pebble.

"Face it," said Hannie. "Scott dumped me."

Hannie was the first person I knew who had been dumped.

We reached Hannie's house. "I'm going to go lie down for awhile," she said.

"Okay." I watched Hannie walk across her front yard. "Sorry the wedding is off!" I called after her.

That was too bad. Now when Mommy and Daddy got married again, they couldn't have a double wedding.

Help From Nannie

Usually David Michael calls me either "Karen" or "Professor." He calls me "Professor" because of my glasses. It is a nice nickname, not a mean one. But on Saturday he didn't call me anything except "greedy-guts." He called me that so many times that Nannie told him to stop it.

I smiled at Nannie. Nannie had not said a word to me about my birthday or my invitations or the list of two hundred and twelve presents. She hadn't called me names like David Michael had. She hadn't frowned at me like Kristy had.

Maybe Nannie wasn't angry with me. Maybe I could talk to her about my birthday. I decided it would be safe to try.

After supper on Saturday, I found Nannie. She was in the den. The TV was on, but Nannie wasn't looking at it. She was looking at her knitting.

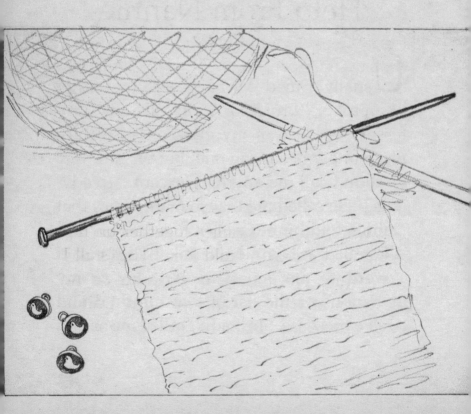

"Hi," I said. I settled myself on the couch next to Nannie. "What are you making?"

"A sweater for Emily," Nannie replied. "Do you think she'll like it?"

I nodded. "Nannie?"

"Yes?"

"I think people are mad at me about my birthday."

"Do you?"

"Yeah."

Nannie didn't sound mad. And she wasn't accusing me of anything. Maybe I could tell her about my families. She might understand.

"You know why I sent out the invitations?" I said.

"No. Why?" replied Nannie. She put her knitting down and looked at me.

"I want my two families together on my birthday this year," I told her. "That's all I *really* want. Not parties or presents or the circus or anything. Mommy and Daddy always seem mad at each other these days.

Either they don't talk, or they have arguments over the phone. And I don't want that. I want Mommy and Daddy and Seth and Elizabeth and you and my brothers and sisters — all of them — together.''

"Oh, Karen.'' Nannie put her arm around me. "Your mommy and daddy aren't mad at each other. Just a little cross. And they're very busy. They each have their own family now. Plus we have Emily Michelle, and your mommy has her job. Even if that weren't true, though, I'm not sure that bringing your two families together would be a good idea. They are two families for a reason. Seth and Elizabeth would feel uncomfortable around each other. No, it's just not a good idea. And it isn't going to happen, Karen. I'm sorry, but it isn't.''

I nodded. Maybe deep down I had known all along that it wouldn't happen. "What should I do now?'' I asked Nannie.

"Well, if you can't have your two families together for your birthday, what do you want instead?''

"Mommy's party at home, and Daddy's circus party. Just what they suggested."

"Okay. And how about presents?"

"I don't really want two hundred and twelve. I just made up that list because I knew Daddy would call Mommy and then they'd have to talk to each other. I only want the first five things on the list."

"Okay," said Nannie. "I'll tell your father for you. But I won't tell him why you made the long list."

"Thank you, Nannie." I kissed her goodnight. Then I went upstairs to bed.

I fell asleep thinking that I used to feel lucky to be a two-two. Now I wished I were a one-one.

Help From Seth

On Sunday night, Andrew and I went back to the little house. Nannie had told Daddy about my birthday plans, but it was up to me to tell Mommy.

I decided to talk to Seth first. Seth was like Nannie. He had not said anything to me about my birthday. He did not seem cross or upset.

I caught Seth just as he was about to go into Andrew's room. Andrew was putting out the DO NOT DISTURB sign.

"Seth?" I said. "Can I talk to you for a minute?"

"Sure," replied Seth. He turned to Andrew. "I'll be right in. Just let me talk to Karen first."

Seth and I sat on my bed.

"Seth?" I said. "I know Mommy is angry about my birthday, so I've been thinking. I decided I do want a party here after all. The grown-up kind that she was talking about.

And I only want the first five things on that list, especially the books. That's all." (I couldn't tell Seth about the two families. I decided that would be between Nannie and me.)

"I think your mother will be happy to hear that," Seth said. He gave me a kiss. Then he called Mommy into my room and I told her my news.

Mommy was gigundo happy. "Who do you want to invite?" she asked.

"Just us, like you said. You and Seth and Andrew and me . . . and Emily Junior?"

"I'm not sure a rat would be a good party guest," said Mommy. "Emily Junior doesn't know how to sit still."

I nodded. "Okay. No Emily."

"How about decorations?" asked Mommy.

"Balloons and crepe paper," I said. I was beginning to feel a little excited. "A big bunch of balloons over my place at the table."

"And food? You can have anything you want."

That was easy. "Hamburgers, mashed potatoes, cake, and ice cream," I said.

"Terrific," Mommy replied. "Vanilla or chocolate cake?"

"Chocolate. And peppermint-stick ice cream."

"Seth!" Andrew called just then. "Come help me with Karen's — I mean, come help me!"

Seth grinned. "I better go. Andrew and I are working on an important project."

Seth left Mommy and me alone. "I'm so glad you changed your mind, Karen," said Mommy. "I think you are really growing up."

Curious Karen

"**O**nly two more days until my birthday! Only two more days until my birthday!" I sang.

I could hardly wait. It seemed like forever since my sixth birthday. And now that I'd decided to have the parties that Mommy and Daddy wanted, I felt better. I had wanted my two families together — but not if everyone was going to be mad.

It was Thursday. School was over. "Just think," I said to Andrew. "In two days you will get to go to the Happy-Time Circus. What are you going to wear?"

"Wear?" Andrew repeated. "Clothes."

"Anything special?"

"I don't know." Andrew was busy with his cars and trucks.

I couldn't believe he hadn't planned his circus outfit. I had planned my circus outfit, the outfit for Mommy's fancy party, and the outfit for my class party in school. This is what I was going to wear:

School party: baggy shirt, red-and-white-striped skirt

Mommy's party: fancy yellow dress, ribbons in my hair

Circus party: blue jeans, unicorn sweat shirt

Daddy and I had sent out invitations for the circus party. We had found ones with clowns and balloons on them. I had invited Andrew, everyone in the big-house family,

Hannie, Nancy, Scott Hsu (he was Hannie's idea; she wanted to be friends with him again), and three other kids. The circus was going to be very, very fun.

I was so excited that I was getting ants in my pants. That's what my big brother Sam would say. How, I wondered, could I wait until my first party the next day? How could I wait until the next night to open some presents? I couldn't. That was all there was to it.

"Andrew?" I said. "Where's Mommy?"

"Next door with Nancy's mommy," he replied. "Vroom, vroom." Andrew never even looked up from his cars and trucks.

Well, this was perfect. It was time to do a little present-hunting. I did that before my last birthday, and just before Christmas, too.

The first place I looked was under Mommy and Seth's bed. Nothing.

Then I looked in Seth's closet. Yea! On the floor was a present. The card read, "For Karen, from Seth. Happy birthday, seven-year-old!" Okay. Now I had to be very careful. Sneaking a peek at presents is not easy. Often, adults can figure out if you have done this. But I am an expert.

I slid the ribbon off to one side without untying it. Then I peeled back a piece of tape — very, very carefully. The end of the package came undone. I looked inside. A book! I peeled away some more tape. The book was *Matilda*, by Roald Dahl! Then, just as carefully, I put the paper back where it

had been, stuck the tape down again, and slid the ribbon on. Pretty good. I didn't think anyone would ever know the present had been peeked at.

Before Mommy came home, I found and opened the rest of my presents — except for Andrew's. He must have hidden it very well. I did find a box under his bed that said LOOK IN HERE in Seth's handwriting, but I didn't look. I knew it was a trick.

Anyway, Mommy was giving me the stuffed ostrich, the plaid bow for my hair, and some clothes. Goody! Now I really couldn't wait until the next night.

Having birthdays is so much fun. When I turned seven, David Michael and I would be the same age at last. And I would be the same age as the other kids in my class. (I am the youngest, since I skipped a grade.)

"Oh, tomorrow, tomorrow," I sang. "Please hurry up and get here!"

The School Party

T omorrow *finally* came. Now it was today. It was the day of Mommy's party, and it was the day of my party in Ms. Colman's class!

Just as I had planned, I wore my baggy shirt and my red-and-white-striped skirt to school. I tied a red ribbon in my hair. On my feet I wore my party shoes. They are shiny and black. Usually I am not allowed to wear them to school, but Mommy said that my birthday was a special occasion.

School is over at 2:45. On my birthday, Mommy was going to come at one-thirty and we were going to spend the rest of the day having a party. Mommy was going to bring cupcakes.

Waiting until one-thirty was very, very hard for me. It was hard for Hannie and Nancy and the other kids in my class, too. We were going to play games and eat, and Ms. Colman said she had a special treat for us. I bet everyone was gigundo glad it was my birthday.

I know I was.

At one-thirty on the dot, I heard a knock on our classroom door.

"My mom is here!" I cried. "That's her! I know it is! She's got the cupcakes!"

"Karen, settle down," said Ms. Colman gently.

I sat quietly at my desk while Ms. Colman opened the door. There stood Mommy with the box of cupcakes and — *Andrew*. Andrew? What was he doing? He wasn't invited. Little brothers aren't supposed to come to class parties.

Andrew followed Mommy into the room, looking shy. A couple of kids nudged each other and pointed at him, but they didn't have a chance to say anything. That was because Ms. Colman said, "It's time for the party to begin! The first thing we're going to do is the surprise. We're going to make hats!"

Ms. Colman and Mommy helped us to make pointy party hats. We decorated the hats with glitter and feathers. I printed BIRTHDAY GIRL on mine with a special pen that wrote in sparkles. Even Andrew made a hat.

Then Ms. Colman said, "Time for refreshments!" We sat at our desks. (Andrew sat with me.) Mommy and Ms. Colman passed out napkins, cups for juice, party blowers, and the cupcakes. Darn old Ricky Torres blew his party favor in my face. I blew mine back in his face. I started to call him, "Yicky

Ricky," but just then Mommy stuck a candle in my cupcake. She lit it and everyone sang "Happy Birthday." Then I blew the candle out.

I just love having people sing to me.

We ate the cupcakes. Yum! Mommy had decorated them to look like cats. I ate my cat's nose first, then the rest of his face, then the rest of the frosting, and finally the cake part.

When we were done eating, we played Pin-the-Tail-on-the-Donkey. Guess who won? Andrew! He won fair and square.

"Boy, he's good," said Ricky Torres.

I felt proud of Andrew. "My brother is good at lots of things," I said. I decided I was glad he had come to my party.

When the bell rang, everyone was sorry. Usually we like the end of the week, but not that day. We were having fun.

I had something to look forward to, though — Mommy's party!

Mommy's Party

That night, Seth came home early for my party. "I need time to get ready," he said. "This is a formal party, so I have to dress up. Andrew, are you going to dress up, too? I'm going to wear my suit."

Andrew hates wearing his suit, but he did not want to be the only person at our party who wasn't dressed up, so he said, "Okay."

Everyone went to their rooms to change their clothes. I put on my fancy yellow dress, the one with a lot of lace on it. Then

I put on my white tights and my black party shoes. Just like I had planned, I tied yellow ribbons in my hair. But first I brushed my hair over and over and over to make sure it was shiny and there were no tangles.

When I was dressed I went downstairs. Mommy was waiting in the living room. She was wearing a dress that so far she had only worn to grown-up parties. It is black and has beads on it.

"Mommy, you look so pretty!" I exclaimed.

"Thank you," said Mommy, kissing me. "Happy birthday, Karen."

Andrew and Seth came downstairs in their suits. Andrew was even wearing his bowtie. It is not a real bowtie. If you pull it, it will come off of his shirt.

"Shall we have drinks and hors d'oeuvres in the living room first?" asked Mommy.

Ooh. Drinks and hors d'oeuvres. This really was a grown-up party.

Mommy poured ginger ale for each of us. Then she passed around potato chips and a plate with carrot sticks, celery sticks, and olives on it. I ate an olive and felt as if I were *much* older than almost seven. I even remembered to put the pit in my napkin where no one could see it.

"Now," said Seth, "it is dinnertime."

Mommy and Seth and Andrew and I walked into the dining room. The lights were off. Candles were burning on the table. Mommy was letting us use real china and real silver. A bunch of pink balloons was hanging over my place. In the middle of the table was a bouquet of flowers.

"This is so fancy!" I said in a whisper.

We ate hamburgers and mashed potatoes, and Mommy and Seth ate some salad. Then it was time for . . . the birthday cake!

Mommy carried it out of the kitchen.

"Happy birthday to you!" sang my little-house family.

The cake was covered with frosting flowers. Andrew and I each got a pink rose. The pink roses matched the peppermint-stick ice cream.

"Well," said Mommy when we were all stuffed, "I think it's time for — "

"Presents?" I asked.

Mommy nodded.

"Hurray! Hurray!" I got out of my chair and began jumping up and down.

"Karen," said Mommy. (I knew she meant "Cool it.")

I opened my presents in the living room. There were the ostrich, the bow, the new clothes, and *Matilda*. I acted very surprised,

and no one guessed that I had already peeked at the presents.

Then Andrew said, "Time for *my* present!"

"I'll help you get it," said Seth.

Andrew and Seth went upstairs. They came down carrying the box that said LOOK IN HERE.

"Is your present really in there?" I asked.

"Yup," said Andrew.

Huh. I never would have guessed.

Inside the box was a playground for Emily Junior. Andrew and Seth had *made* it. That's why Andrew had been hanging the DO NOT DISTURB sign on his door.

"See?" said Andrew. "There's a maze and a tunnel and a seesaw. Now Emily Junior will never get bored."

"Thanks, Andrew," I said. I gave him a hug. I didn't tell anybody, but I liked Andrew's present the best of all.

The Circus Party

Later that evening, Mommy and Seth drove Andrew and me to the big house. My little-house party was over. The next day would be . . . circus day!

Saturday was my actual birthday. It was the day I would *really* turn seven. When I woke up on Saturday, the sun was shining and the sky was blue. It was perfect birthday weather!

At noon, my friends began arriving at the big house.

"Happy birthday, Karen!" they cried. They

all brought presents. We put the presents in the living room. Then we climbed into cars to go to the circus. There were so many of us that we needed four cars — Daddy's, Elizabeth's, Charlie's, and Nannie's.

We drove to Stamford. Every now and then, someone would see a sign for the Happy-Time Circus, and we would cheer.

"We're almost there!" I shouted.

The Happy-Time Circus was an indoor circus, not an outdoor circus under a tent. We drove to a big building and parked the cars in a garage. Then we went inside the building. Daddy reached in his pocket and pulled out an envelope. It held the circus tickets. He handed them to a man, and we followed a crowd of people into an arena.

"Ooh," I said softly. "Is this the circus?"

"It's going to be," replied Daddy.

We were standing in one of the hugest places I've ever seen. And we were way up high. Below us, on the floor, were three rings. Above us were the tightropes and trapeze bars. We found our seats, and for a few moments we were quiet.

I noticed that all around us, kids were waving fancy flashlights. Some of them looked like tigers, some like sparkly fairy dust. Daddy bought us each a flashlight.

"Can we get popcorn?" I asked.

"Or cotton candy?" asked Andrew.

"No food," said Daddy. "Wait until we're home. We'll have a special treat then."

We waited patiently for the circus to start. Hannie was sitting next to me. On her other side was Scott Hsu.

"Are you going to get married?" I asked her.

Hannie shook her head. "Not yet. Scott has to fall in love with me first." Hannie turned to Scott. "Scott?" she said. "Here. You can have my flashlight, okay?"

"Really?" Scott replied. "Boy, thanks!" Scott grinned at Hannie.

Hannie grinned at me.

Soon the arena grew dark. We waved our flashlights around. The ringmaster stepped into the center ring. "Welcome to the Happy-Time Circus!" he said. "Today you will see the world's most exciting show — clowns and animals, death-defying acts high above your head, jugglers and tumblers and more."

The show began. A cowboy clown chased another cowboy clown around and around the center ring. They shot at each other with cap guns. (The guns made Emily Michelle cry). One clown pushed the other onto a piano with a *crash!*

We laughed and laughed.

We watched Paddy's Trained Poodles and Biff's Trained Bears. We saw a parade of elephants. We saw white horses. We saw the Cecily Sisters turn somersaults in the air using the trapeze.

"How do they do that?" I asked Hannie.

She didn't answer. She was watching a woman selling ice cream. "Can we get some ice cream?" she asked Daddy.

"Sorry," said Daddy. "Wait until we're home. We'll have plenty to eat there."

"Boo," whispered Hannie.

"If I had any money," said Scott, "I'd buy you *two* ice creams, Hannie."

Hannie grinned again.

We settled back to watch the rest of the show. I decided I liked the clowns best.

After the Circus

After the circus I rode home in Daddy's car. Andrew, Hannie, Scott, and Sam were with us. "Quick!" said Daddy. "Everybody tell me your favorite part of the circus!"

"The clowns," I said.

"Yeah, the cowboy clowns," agreed Scott.

"The pretty lady clowns," said Hannie.

"My flashlight," said Andrew.

"The gorilla," said Sam.

"What gorilla?" I asked.

"Just testing you," said Sam. He is such a tease.

When we reached our house, Nannie showed everyone into the dining room. We sat down at the table. Hannie sat next to Scott. My friends and I put on party hats and waited.

Soon the door to the kitchen opened. In came Daddy. He was carrying a big cake. "Happy birthday to you!" everyone sang. Daddy set the cake in front of me. I counted seven candles and one to grow on.

The cake looked like the circus. It was decorated with clowns and acrobats and elephants. Daddy and Nannie served the cake. My piece had a clown face on it!

"Eat up!" said Daddy, so we ate our cake and ice cream.

Then it was time for presents. I sat on the couch in the living room. The presents were stacked next to me.

"Open mine first!" said Hannie.

So I did. Inside was a stuffed elephant. "To remind you of the circus," said Hannie.

"Thanks!" I exclaimed. "I'll name him Babar."

I opened the rest of the presents. Every
now and then I glanced at Hannie and Scott.
They were always together. When the party
was over, Hannie whispered to me as she
was leaving, "I asked Scott to marry me
again, and this time he said, 'Yes.' I am so
happy!"

"I'm happy, too," I told her. "I can't wait
for the wedding!"

Hannie was the last guest to leave. When
she was gone, I looked around the living

room at my gifts and the wrapping paper and ribbon.

"Do you want to open your family presents now?" asked Daddy.

"Could I wait until tomorrow?" I replied. "That way I can stretch out my birthday."

"Sure," said Daddy, "but honestly, Karen, I have never seen anyone make such a big deal over her birthday as you."

"Big deal?" I repeated.

"Yes," said Daddy. "Two hundred and twelve presents, a huge party."

"Turning seven is exciting," I said.

"Maybe," replied Daddy. "But you can celebrate your birthday without being greedy."

So Daddy still thought I was greedy. I knew the time had come to tell him the truth. I would have to say it even if it was very, very hard.

"Daddy," I began, "I didn't really want two hundred and twelve presents. I just knew that if I asked for them you would have to call Mommy and talk to her. You never talk to each other anymore. And I wanted the big party so you and Mommy would be together. Andrew and I like to see you together. We . . . we want you to get married again."

"Oh, Karen," said Daddy. He opened his arms for a hug. "That's not going to happen," he told me. "We're each married to other people now. And we're each happily married."

"I know," I said. I didn't understand *why* it was so. But I knew that that was the way things were.

The Surprise

Daddy and I talked for a long time that night. I told him I wished that he and Mommy would call each other just a little more often, and *not* fight so often. I told him again how much Andrew and I missed seeing him and Mommy together. And I told him how bad I felt when he and Mommy "forgot" me at school after the field trip.

Guess what happened then?

Daddy called Mommy. And he didn't even make me leave the kitchen. He let me stay and listen to the phone conversation.

"Hi, Lisa," he said. "It's Watson. . . . No, nothing's wrong. We had a great day. The circus was fun — "

"We saw clowns!" I shouted.

"Did you hear that?" asked Daddy. "That was Karen telling you we saw clowns. And elephants and trained animals and a lot of other things. Anyway, Karen and I just had a little talk." Daddy told Mommy everything we'd discussed. "So I think," he went on, "that we should make an effort to stay in touch more. After all, Karen and Andrew are still *our* children. Our children *together*, despite the divorce." Mommy must have agreed with Daddy because the next thing Daddy said was, "I'm glad you feel that way. Okay, we'll see you tomorrow."

When Daddy hung up the phone I was grinning. I bet my smile was a mile wide. "Thank you!" I cried.

The next day I waited all morning and part of the afternoon to open my family presents. Finally I said, "Okay, I'm ready!"

"Really?" said Sam. "Are you sure you don't want to wait until next year and open them when you turn eight?"

"Sa-am!" I cried. "No!"

"Or you could wait until you're twelve. Then you could open six years' worth of presents at once. It would probably take you a whole day."

"No!" I cried. "Now!" But I knew Sam was just teasing again.

Everyone scattered to get the presents they'd been hiding. (I had not searched for presents at the big house. There were always too many people around.) When everyone came back, I was sitting next to another pile of presents. Daddy gave me the Little Miss Georgine doll. Elizabeth gave me *Charlie and the Chocolate Factory* and *James and the Giant Peach* by Roald Dahl. Kristy gave me another book by Roald Dahl. It was called *The Witches.*

"A whole book about witches!" I exclaimed. "Thank you!"

There were presents from everyone (except Andrew). Even Emily gave me a present. It was a piece of paper with a big brown scribble on it.

"Emmy," she said. "Rat."

It was a picture of Emily Junior.

"Oh, it's beautiful!" I cried. "I'll hang it up in my room here."

Emily smiled. She was very pleased with herself.

But the best surprise was when Mommy and Seth arrived to pick up Andrew and me. They came right inside. They looked at my presents. They told Emily how nice her picture was. They listened to me tell about the circus party.

Then Mommy said, "Karen, Daddy and I had a talk. We want you to know we will never 'forget' you again. And from now on, we will listen to you more carefully. Deal?"

"Deal!" I cried.

I had given up on their wedding. I knew it wouldn't happen. Seth and Elizabeth were standing right in front of me and they were part of my family. No, my *two* families, I

corrected myself. I had *two* families and that wouldn't change.

I thought about my birthday — the parties and cakes and presents and the circus. You know what the best part was? It was right now. It was my two families together, even if it was for just a few minutes.

About the Author

ANN M. MARTIN lives in New York City and loves animals. Her cat, Mouse, knows how to take the phone off the hook.

Other books by Ann M. Martin that you might enjoy are *Stage Fright*, *Me and Katie (the Pest)*, and the books in *The Baby-sitters Club* series.

Ann likes ice cream, the beach, and *I Love Lucy*. And she has her own little sister, whose name is Jane.

Little Sister

Don't miss #8

KAREN'S HAIRCUT

I sat down in the haircutting chair. I was so excited. I could feel the butterflies in my tummy. Gloriana began to snip away.

Gloriana had been cutting my hair for a while when Mommy came over to me and said, "Andrew is getting wiggly. I'm going to take him for a walk, okay?"

"Okay," I answered.

While Mommy and Andrew were gone, Gloriana snipped and cut and cut and snipped. My long hair fell in a pile on the floor. Suddenly I realized something awful. My hair was getting too short! But I was afraid to tell Gloriana.

I wanted Mommy.

By the time Mommy and Andrew came back, Gloriana was finished with my hair. It was not the cut I had asked for.

I was practically bald.

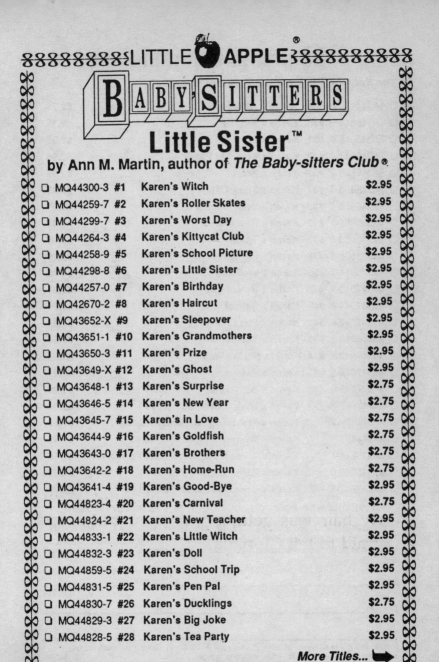

LITTLE APPLE ®

BABY-SITTERS
Little Sister™
by Ann M. Martin, author of *The Baby-sitters Club* ®

More Titles... ➡

888888888888888888888888888888888888

The Baby-sitters Little Sister titles continued...

☐	MQ44825-0	#29	Karen's Cartwheel	$2.75
☐	MQ45645-8	#30	Karen's Kittens	$2.75
☐	MQ45646-6	#31	Karen's Bully	$2.95
☐	MQ45647-4	#32	Karen's Pumpkin Patch	$2.95
☐	MQ45648-2	#33	Karen's Secret	$2.95
☐	MQ45650-4	#34	Karen's Snow Day	$2.95
☐	MQ45652-0	#35	Karen's Doll Hospital	$2.95
☐	MQ45651-2	#36	Karen's New Friend	$2.95
☐	MQ45653-9	#37	Karen's Tuba	$2.95
☐	MQ45655-5	#38	Karen's Big Lie	$2.95
☐	MQ45654-7	#39	Karen's Wedding	$2.95
☐	MQ47040-X	#40	Karen's Newspaper	$2.95
☐	MQ47041-8	#41	Karen's School	$2.95
☐	MQ47042-6	#42	Karen's Pizza Party	$2.95
☐	MQ46912-6	#43	Karen's Toothache	$2.95
☐	MQ47043-4	#44	Karen's Big Weekend	$2.95
☐	MQ47044-2	#45	Karen's Twin	$2.95
☐	MQ47045-0	#46	Karen's Baby-sitter	$2.95
☐	MQ43647-3		Karen's Wish Super Special #1	$2.95
☐	MQ44834-X		Karen's Plane Trip Super Special #2	$3.25
☐	MQ44827-7		Karen's Mystery Super Special #3	$2.95
☐	MQ45644-X		Karen's Three Musketeers Super Special #4	$2.95
☐	MQ45649-0		Karen's Baby Super Special #5	$3.25
☐	MQ46911-8		Karen's Campout Super Special #6	$3.25

Available wherever you buy books, or use this order form.

888888888888888888888888888888888888